This book
belongs
to

C. O'Sullivan

by Nancy White Carlstrom

The Snow Speaks

Illustrated by Jane Dyer

Little, Brown and Company
Boston Toronto London

Special thanks to Barry Moser for driving the snowplow

Text copyright © 1992 by Nancy White Carlstrom
Illustrations copyright © 1992 by Jane Dyer

First Edition

Library of Congress Cataloging-in-Publication Data

Carlstrom, Nancy White.
    The snow speaks / by Nancy White Carlstrom; illustrated by Jane
    Dyer. — 1st ed.
       p. cm.
    Summary: Captures the sights and sounds of the season's first
    snowfall.
    ISBN 0-316-12861-9
    [1. Snow—fiction.] I. Dyer, Jane, ill. II. Title.
    PZ7.C21684Sn 1992
    [E]—dc20   91-36141

    10 9 8 7 6 5 4 3 2 1

NIL

Published simultaneously in Canada
by Little, Brown & Company (Canada) Limited

Printed in Italy by New Interlitho S.p.A. - Milan

For Mom and Dad Carlstrom
— N. W. C.
For Cecily, my snow child
— J. D.

As the first white flakes blow
softly to earth
and the children's faces
fill the window with longing,
The snow speaks out a greeting:
Hello Hello Hello,
as if it has just come to visit.

But the children know
it is here to stay.

When words freeze
   in the thin, brittle air
   and nostrils stick together,
The snow speaks
   in squeaks and crunches
   under the children's feet.
Cold Cold Cold

The children know this stubborn snow
 will not be held within
 a snowman's shape.
It is light as feathers,
 endless as a winter sky.

When the old yellow plow
   swerves along the curve of road
   like a ship at sea,
   leaving the mailbox adrift,
   mouth open wide,
The snow speaks in waves and spray
   as bold as salt sea air.
Blow Blow Blow

The children know
   they must shake out the letters
   and stay buttoned, hooded,
   mittened, zipped.

When the snowshoe hare
    hops in a line by the cedar fence
    and birds step lightly
    on little stick feet,
The snow speaks in scratches and tracks
    on its fine white back.
Look Look Look

The children know if they use
their wise, patient eyes,
They can read other secrets
of the snow.

When the moon fills the sky
    and the trees all around with light,
The snow speaks in sparkling stars
    on the firm, sure crust.
Shine Shine Shine

The children know there is magic
in these woods.
The snow told them.

Then deep winter sets in.
Day climbs into night
for one long, winding darkness.
And there is snow on snow on snow.

The children know they must stay inside
by the fire,
warmed and waiting. Tired.

Just when the snow seems forever silent
in the dark, drear night,
muffled whispers break the spell.

Trapped snow angels
grow and grow and swell to life, singing,
Glory! Glory! Glory!

Then the children know
the snow
speaks Christmas.